P9-CLR-482

The Magic Tapestry

A Chinese folktale retold and illustrated by

Henry Holt • New York

Henry Holt and Company, Inc.
Publishers since 1866
115 West 18th Street
New York, New York 10011

Henry Holt is a registered trademark of
Henry Holt and Company, Inc.

Published in Canada by Fitzhenry & Whiteside Ltd.,
195 Allstate Parkway, Markham, Ontario L3R 4T8.

Library of Congress Cataloging-in-Publication Data
Demi.
The magic tapestry: a Chinese folktale / retold and
illustrated by Demi.
Summary: The youngest of three sons must
overcome frightening obstacles to win back his
mother's heavenly tapestry, stolen by the fairies of Sun Mountain.
[1. Fairy tales. 2. Folklore—China.] I. Title.
PZ8.D379Mag 1994 398.21—dc20 [E] 93-11426

ISBN 0-8050-2810-2

First Edition—1994

Printed in the United States of America
on acid-free paper. ∞

1 2 3 4 5 6 7 8 9 10

Long ago, a poor widow and her three sons lived in southern China. She was a weaver, as her mother and grandmother had been before her. But she had a special gift. She could weave the most beautiful tapestries of all.

Month after month, day after day, she worked on her loom. The two older sons began to complain, "Mother, now you weave all the time but never sell anything. We are tired of chopping wood to support you."

"I must finish this tapestry," replied the widow.

The youngest son understood his mother's heart, so he alone went up to the mountain every day and chopped enough wood for the whole family.

A year passed. The poor woman kept weaving every day. And she wove every night by the light of burning pine branches. The smoke hurt her eyes so much they became red. But still she would not stop. When her tears began to drop on her work, she wove them into the fabric as a clear flowing river and a crystal pool for fish.

Another year passed and her reddened eyes began to bleed. She wove these tears of blood into the fabric as rays of the sun and petals of crimson flowers.

Still, she kept on weaving day and night. Then at the end of the third year the mother went to her sons and declared, "My work is finished!" And there it all was—the most heavenly tapestry ever made. Flowers shimmered with threads of brilliant sunlight and little animals danced magically throughout the woven pattern. The tapestry seemed to breathe with life.

Suddenly, when the older sons began to argue over who would sell the tapestry, a great wind blew in the window from the west. And *swish*—away went the tapestry out the door! Everyone chased after it, but it was blown too high. And then it vanished into the eastern sky.

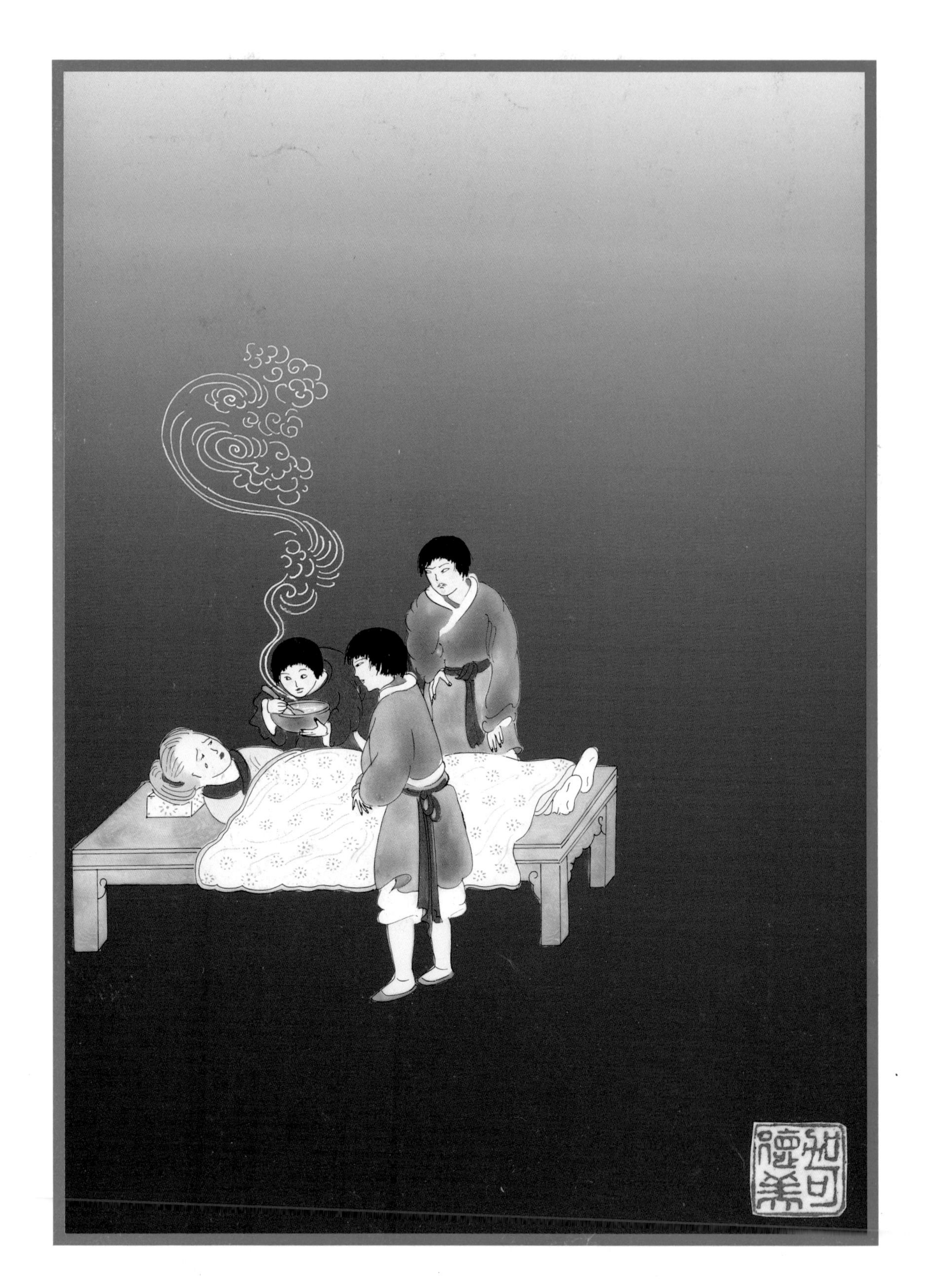

The poor mother fainted. Her youngest son carried her into the house and laid her on a little wooden bed. He gently revived his mother with warm ginger soup, while the older sons only wailed at the loss of their fortune.

"Go, find my tapestry!" the mother pleaded with her eldest son as she opened her eyes. "It means more to me than life itself."

Reluctantly, the eldest son set out for the east.

He traveled for more than a month. Finally, in a remote mountain pass, he came upon a fantastic Dragon Tower. Guarding the tower was a fierce protector spirit, and standing nearby was a stone horse.

"Where are you going?" demanded the guardian.

"To find my mother's tapestry," replied the son.

"That heavenly tapestry was whisked away by the fairies of Sun Mountain so that they could weave copies of it," explained the guardian.

"You can get the tapestry back, but it will be very difficult. First you must knock out your two front teeth and place them in my horse's mouth. He will come to life and eat these magic apples. If you dare, ride him to Sun Mountain.

"First, you will have to pass through the Mountain of Fire. If you utter the slightest complaint, you will instantly be burned to ashes. Then you will have to cross the Sea of Ice, where, if you make the slightest shudder, you will be frozen into a crystal pillar!"

The eldest son's face became as white as a ghost's. The guardian studied him long and hard and then said, "Perhaps you would rather have a box of jewels!"

The guardian held out a box of fabulous jewels. The eldest son took the treasure and left without saying a word.

On his way home, the eldest son thought aloud, "Why should I share these with my family?"

So he didn't go home. Instead, he went to the city and kept all the jewels for himself.

His mother waited for him patiently. When he didn't return, her eyes became weary with tears. She begged her second son to go and find the tapestry.

When the second son reached the mountain pass, the guardian told him how to find the tapestry. And like his brother before him, the second son took the jewels and went to the city.

The mother anxiously awaited her second son. When he didn't return with the tapestry, she went blind from weeping. "Let me go, Mother!" cried the youngest son. "I'll bring back your tapestry, I promise." The poor, blind mother nodded her consent.

Now the youngest son arrived at the mountain pass. There he met the guardian in front of the Dragon Tower.

The guardian told the youngest son how to find the magic tapestry. He looked at the youngest son long and hard, and then he said, "Your brothers each preferred a box of jewels. You may have one too!"

"I have promised to bring back the tapestry," replied the son. "And so I shall."

The youngest son knocked out his two front teeth with a rock and put them into the horse's mouth. The stone horse came to life and ate the magic apples!

Then the horse lifted his head and neighed. The youngest son leapt onto its back and held on tightly as the powerful animal galloped off toward the east.

Through craggy mountain
passes they flew . . .

. . . up and down steep mountain peaks without ever stopping. They came to the Mountain of Fire. The youngest son urged his horse on and bravely went up the mountain.

Flames roared all around him,
but he clenched his fists and
uttered not a sound.

Then they came to the Sea of Ice. Cold waves, surging with ice, rolled and lashed at him.

He was freezing from the bitter cold and aching with pain, but he held on to his horse's mane and showed no fear.

Suddenly, the terrible waves receded and he reached the opposite shore. Before him was Sun Mountain!

Flowers bloomed everywhere in the brilliant sunshine. From a beautiful palace on top of the mountain, peals of musical laughter rang out.

The youngest son spurred his horse on. It leapt into the air . . .

. . . and arrived right at the palace door.

The youngest son entered the palace to find a great hall. In the center of the hall hung his mother's tapestry . . .

. . . and seated at their looms, all around the tapestry, were beautiful fairy princesses busily making copies of it.

"I've come for my mother's tapestry," announced the youngest son.

The startled fairies gathered around him and begged him not to take the tapestry. Then the most beautiful fairy, who was dressed in red, stepped forward. The youngest son looked in her eyes and secretly wished he could stay at Sun Mountain forever. "Please, may we finish our weaving tonight? And in the morning you may take the tapestry to your mother?" The youngest son agreed.

To thank him, the fairies brought him a delicious feast to eat. Then, while he slept, they hung up a brilliant pearl that shone brighter than any lamp and sat down at their looms to work.

The youngest son awoke right before dawn. All the fairies were gone, but his mother's tapestry was neatly rolled and waiting for him under the shining pearl.

Thoughts of the beautiful fairy filled the youngest son's head, but he picked up the tapestry and left the palace. He mounted his horse and galloped off, holding the tapestry next to his heart. He crossed the Sea of Ice and struggled back through the Mountain of Fire. And he never showed any fear.

When he reached the mountain pass, the fierce guardian greeted him warmly. The protector spirit told the youngest son to dismount. He removed the teeth from the horse and placed them in the youngest son's mouth.

The horse turned back to stone. Then the guardian said, "Take these deerskin boots and you will fly safely home."

The youngest son put on the boots and felt himself rise and fly through the air as if he had wings.

The youngest son was home instantly. He ran through the front door and found his mother in her bed.

Helping his mother rise from her bed, he led her outdoors, where he unrolled the magic tapestry on the grass. This time the mother wept tears of joy. The light from the brilliant tapestry healed her eyes in a gentle bath of shining rays.

Suddenly, a fragrant breeze flowed across the tapestry. The tapestry grew bigger and bigger, wider and wider, until it was everywhere—all around the mother and son.

The animals in the tapestry came to life, and beautiful flowers waved in the breeze. Little lambs, rabbits, and calves bounded in and out of the woven grasses and frolicked in the flowers.

The landscape around them was exactly the same as the mother's tapestry. Except for one thing—the beautiful fairy princess dressed in red was there too. She had secretly woven herself into the fabric that night in the palace. And now she was standing in the flowers, waiting for the youngest son to make her his wife.